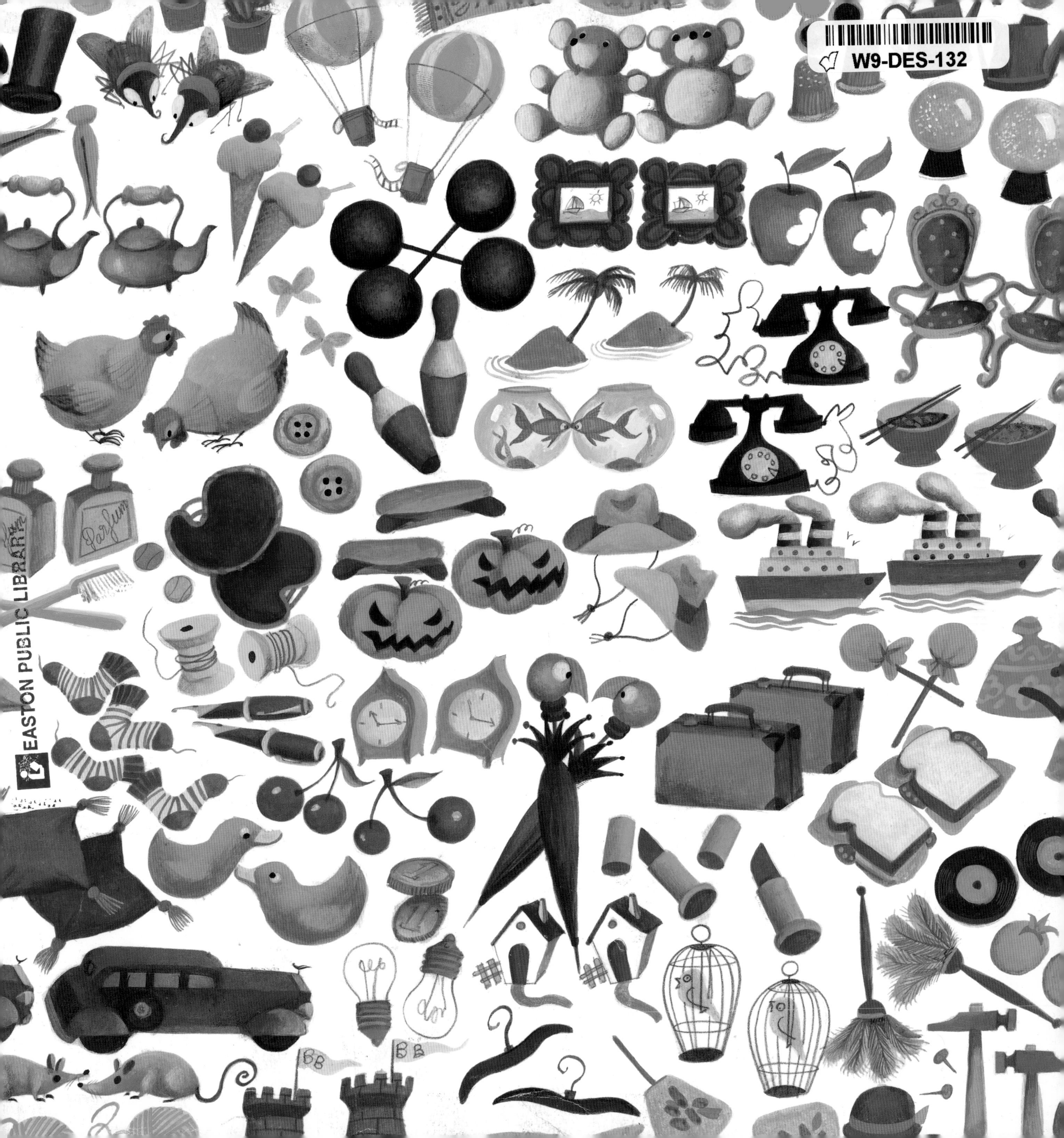
Parfum
BB
BB

For the Thomas family, with love and gratitude.
And with many thanks to Anne Schwartz, who did so
much to bring light and life to this story.
—M. de V.

For my TWO beloved sisters, Pepa and Carmen
—A.J.

Text copyright © 2007 by Monique de Varennes
Illustrations copyright © 2007 by Ana Juan

www.randomhouse.com/kids

Educators and librarians, for a variety of teaching tools, visit us at www.randomhouse.com/teachers

Library of Congress Cataloging-in-Publication Data

Varennes, Monique de.
The jewel box ballerinas / Monique de Varennes ; illustrated by Ana Juan. 1st ed.
p. cm.
Summary: A rich woman purchases a magic jewel box and
sets out to make the two tiny ballerinas within it smile again.
ISBN 978-0-375-83605-3 (trade) ISBN 978-0-375-93605-0 (lib. bdg.)
[1. Magic—Fiction. 2. Friendship—Fiction. 3. Music box—Fiction.]
I. Juan, Ana, ill. II. Title.
PZ7.V427Je 2006
[E]—dc22
2004019622

The text for this book is set in Archetype.
The illustrations are rendered in acrylic and crayon.

PRINTED IN CHINA

1 3 5 7 9 10 8 6 4 2

First Edition

The Jewel Box Ballerinas

MONIQUE DE VARENNES

pictures by
ANA JUAN

schwartz & wade books • new york

There once lived a woman so rich that she had two of almost everything. She had two long limos to whisk her through the streets, two fine houses to choose from every night, and two silly dogs to leap around her feet, yapping at the ends of two silver leashes. When she was in the mood, she even wore two hats, exactly alike, one on top of the other.

Her name was Bibi Branchflower.

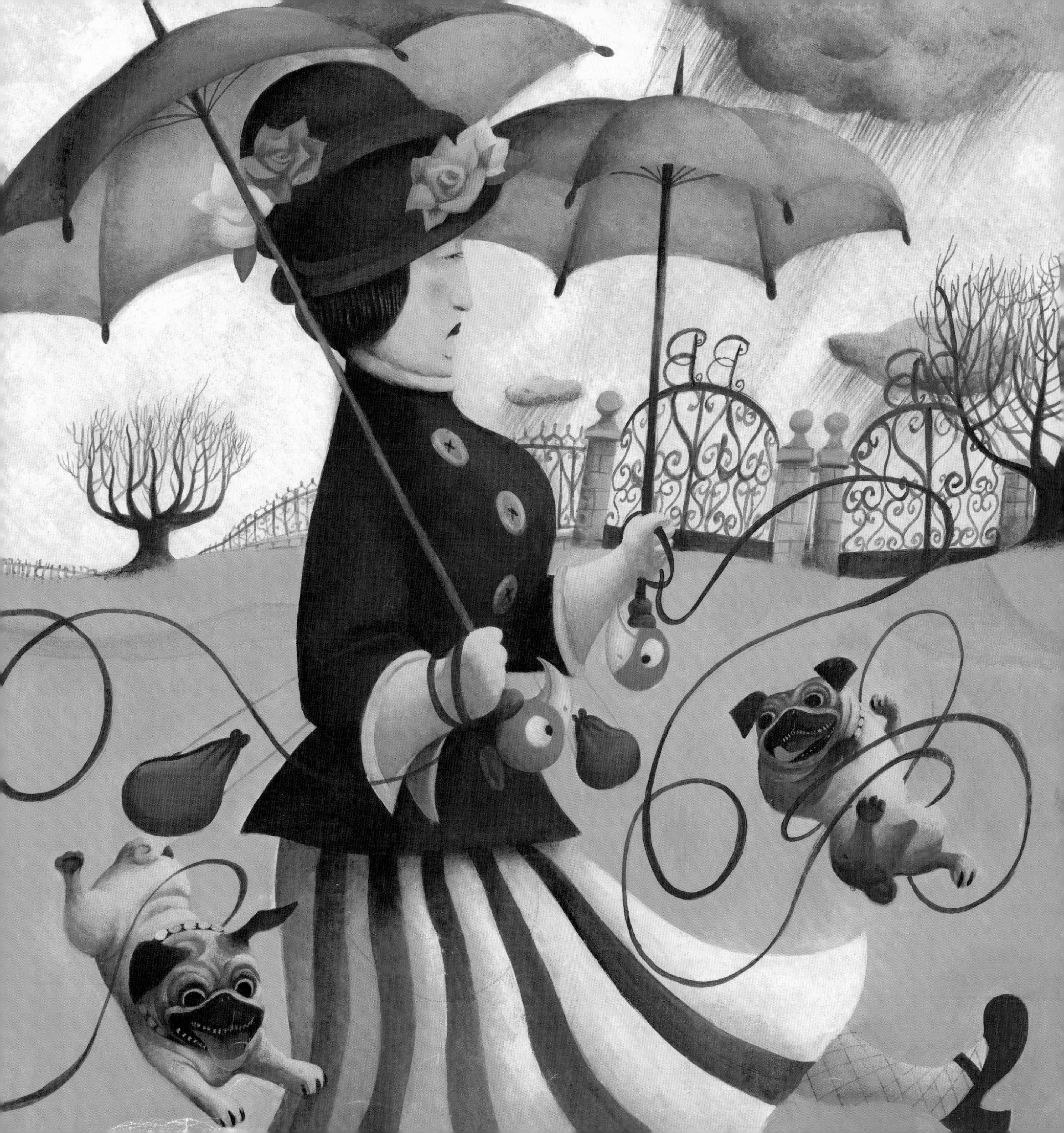

The one thing Bibi did not have was a friend.

Some say she cared so much for cars and fancy clothes that she had no love left for anything else.

One day, in a tiny shop on a crooked street, Bibi saw a beautiful jewel box. It was made of pure gold and studded with precious stones. "Charming!" she said to the shopkeeper. "I'll take two."

"I'm sorry," he replied. "There is just one box like it in all the world."

"But I only buy things in twos," Bibi said, pouting, and she turned to go.

"Wait!" cried the shopkeeper. "Perhaps you will want this after all." And he flung up the lid.

Inside, two glorious ballerinas sprang up and began to spin to the tune of a lively waltz. They were dressed in crimson and wore toe shoes so tiny that Bibi could not guess how they had been made.

"Twins! I must have them!" she exclaimed, reaching out for the box.

But the shopkeeper held it tight. "First, there is something you must know," he whispered.

"Long ago, it is said, a great sorcerer planned a birthday surprise for his twin nieces. They were selfish, foolish girls, but he loved them dearly. He used all his wealth to make this jewel box, and all his powers to create these dancers. Their brilliant smiles glowed like magic.

"But when the sorcerer presented the box, his spoiled nieces ignored it—they had hoped for twin ponies instead. 'You are not worthy of my gift,' he said with tears in his eyes. 'From now on, all who look on these ballerinas will see the sorrow you have caused me.'

"At that very moment, the little dancers lost their smiles. In fact, they look so sad that I've never found a customer who can bear to keep them."

"Piffle!" exclaimed Bibi, trying hard not to look at their faces. "I don't believe a word of it." And pressing gold into the shopkeeper's hand, she seized the box and carried it away.

Despite the shopkeeper's warning,
Bibi was delighted with her ballerinas.

She named them Miranda and Mathilda,
and she opened her jewel box at least twice
a day just to watch them twirl.

She had two tiny costumes made, all in
glittery gold, and laughed out loud when she
learned what ballet skirts were called.
"Two-twos," she beamed. "Perfect!"
She was careful not to look at her
dancers' faces.

But one day, as Bibi bent to change their costumes, she peeked. "Why, it's true," she cried. "You do look terribly sad.

"Still, if you once smiled, surely you can smile again."

Bibi tried everything to cheer her
dancers up. She bought them gifts and
she told them jokes.

She stood on her head for
them and waggled her legs in
the air.

Still their faces drooped
with sadness.

"This is hard!" Bibi exclaimed. She bent close to them and whispered, "What will make you happy, my dear Miranda, my dear Mathilda? I wish you could tell me."

Just as if they had answered, an idea came to Bibi, and for the first time ever, she kissed her lovely girls.

"Is that a smile?" she asked, for it seemed that their faces brightened.

Then she shook her head. "Oh, piffle, it's only my old eyes making a fool of me. All the same, dear dancers, I'll kiss you often, for that felt wonderful indeed."

The very next day, Bibi began to rummage
happily among her jewels.

"We're going on a trip," she told
Miranda and Mathilda, "to Alaska and
Africa. Two different places, and they
both start with *A*!
    "We'll go all through the alphabet
if we have to, till we find a place that
cheers you up."

Bibi plucked her
ballerinas out of the jewel box,
wrapped a silk scarf around them, and pinned the
scarf firmly to her jacket. Their little faces poked out like two
flowers. "There," she said. "Now let's have some adventures."

Their first stop was Alaska. "Br-r-r," Bibi shuddered, "it's shivery cold! But surely something here will make you smile." And cupping her hands around her little dancers to keep them warm, Bibi set off to explore.

She darted up icy blue glaciers and waded through chilly green streams.

She pointed out seals and salmon, beavers and bears. And of course she bought heaps of souvenirs—two of everything.

One morning, when Bibi lifted her dancers from their bed, she cried out in surprise. "You're warm, just as if I'd held you all night! In fact, you feel like real girls." And she kissed them on their pale pink cheeks.

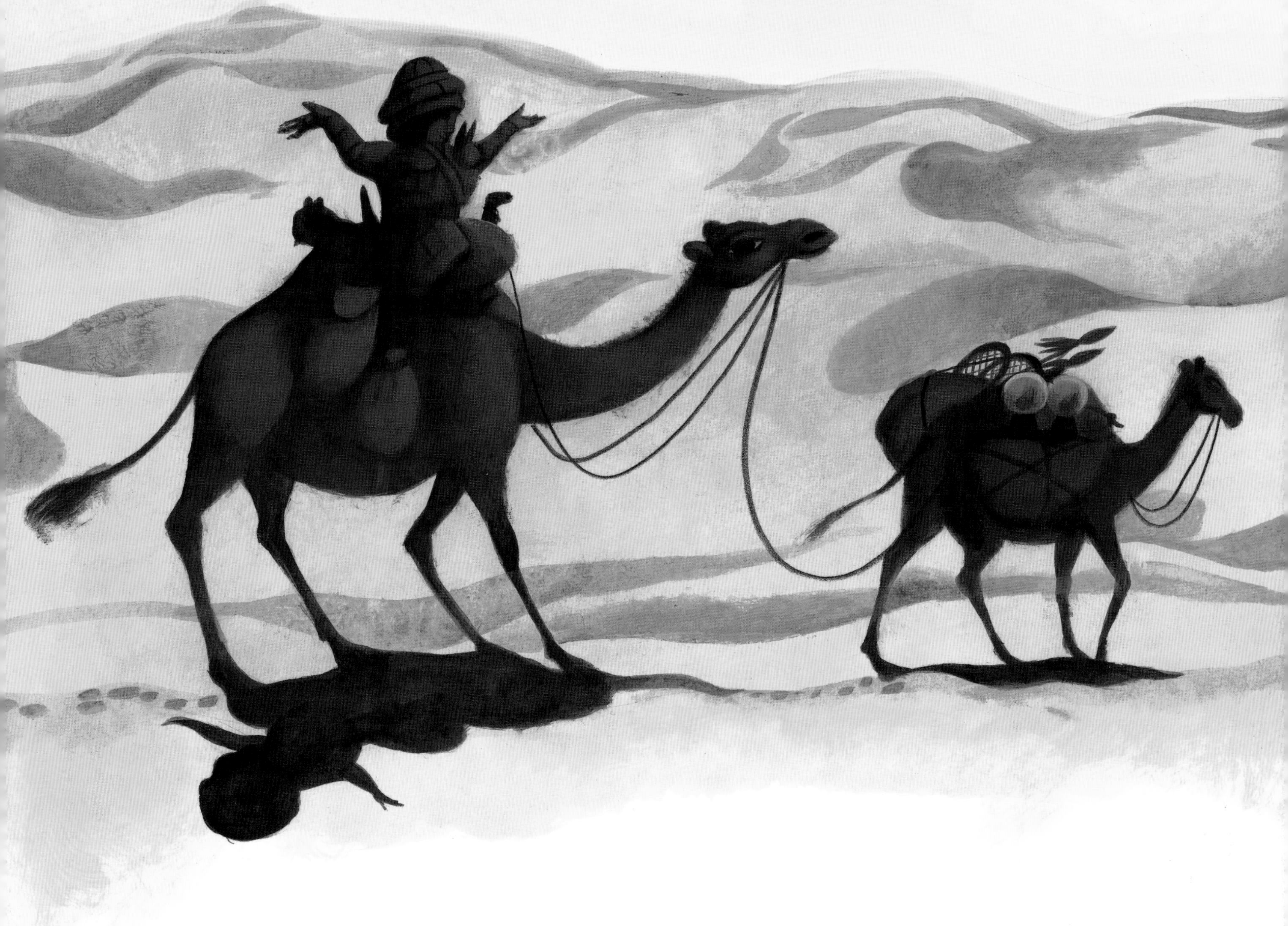

Then on they went to Africa, traveling the great length of the continent. They rode a camel through the golden desert, an elephant through the leafy jungle, and an ostrich through the grasslands of the south. "Much more fun than my two limousines," said Bibi.

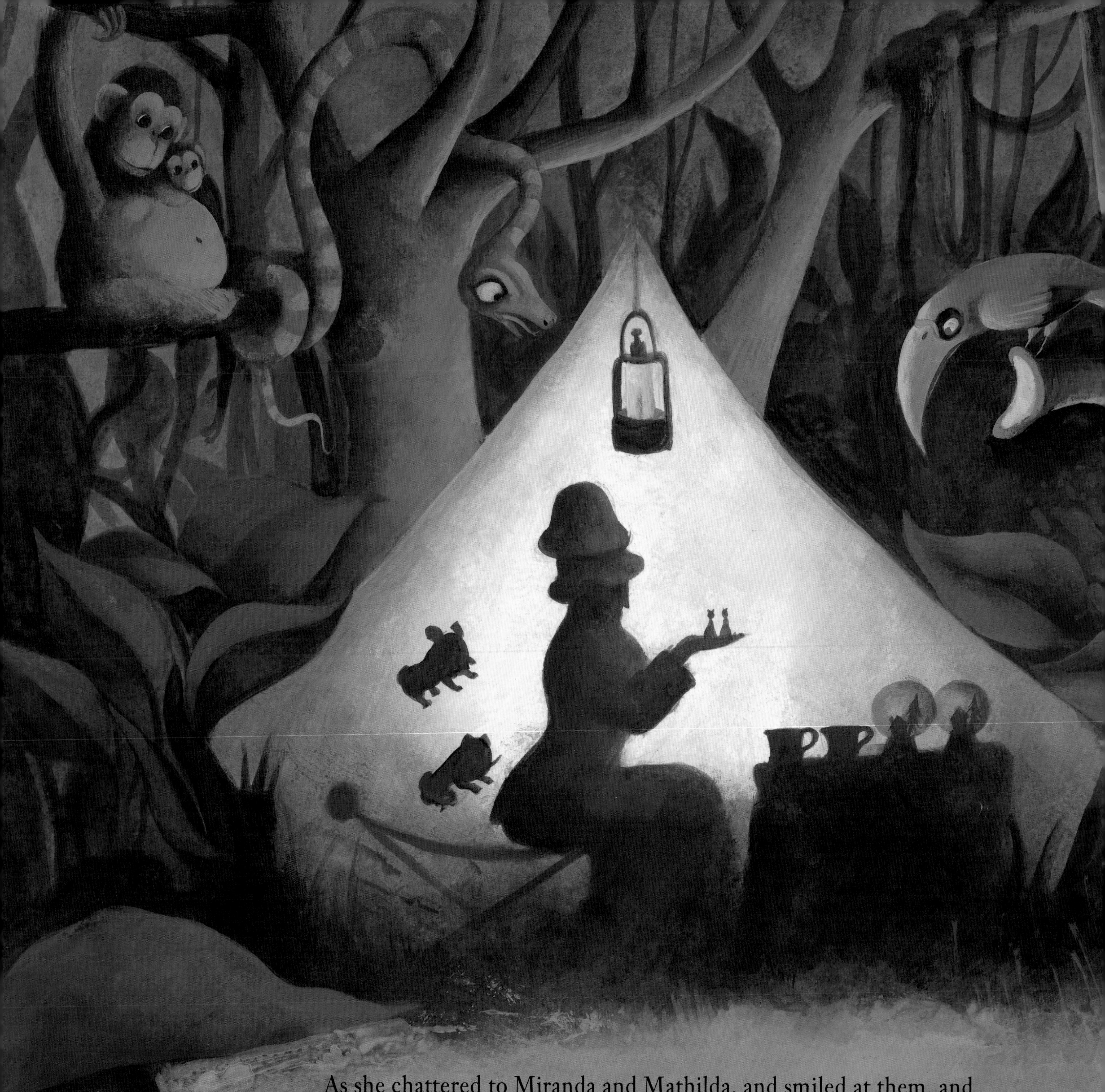

As she chattered to Miranda and Mathilda, and smiled at them, and kissed them, Bibi saw that their faces shone more brightly every day.

"If only you could talk!" said Bibi. "I'd love to have two real friends just like you."

On her last day in Africa, Bibi passed a marketplace. "Oooh, shopping!" she exclaimed, and she bustled from stall to stall, buying two of everything.

Then, while she was looking at some wooden carvings, the knot on her scarf came loose. Out slipped Miranda and Mathilda.

They tumbled to the ground and lay there, looking up at her with worried eyes. But Bibi was too busy to notice.

As she turned to go, two voices floated up to her. "Bibi!" cried one, as clear as water.

"Don't leave us!" cried the other, as light as air.

"Who's that?" wondered Bibi, looking all around. Then she shook her head. "Oh, piffle! It's only my old ears making a fool of me." And she set off for her hotel.

That night Bibi took out all her souvenirs. She put on two furry hats with enormous earflaps, then two safari hats that teetered on top. She set out drums and daggers, statues and snowshoes, until all her treasures towered around her. "What fun we've had, my darling girls," she said, gazing happily into her mirrors.

Bibi peered more closely at her reflection. "Miranda, Mathilda! Where are you?" she gasped. For she saw at last that they were gone.

She scurried around the room, looking everywhere—under the bed, behind the desk, and even in the great gold lamp that dangled from the ceiling. But they were not to be found.

"Don't worry, my sweet ones—I'm coming," Bibi cried. She rushed outside, her hats flying from her head, and hurried through the dark village, searching.

All night she ran, calling her dancers' names.

But there was no answer.

Finally Bibi stopped, too tired to take another step. Her clothes were dusty, her hair stuck out in all directions, and she had lost one shoe. "Oh, Miranda! Oh, Mathilda!" she wailed. "What will I do without you? I'd give up all I own to have you back again!"

Just at that moment, dawn touched the skies, and in the hazy light, Bibi saw two tiny figures standing far up the road. It was Miranda and Mathilda.

"My darlings!" cried Bibi, and she ran toward them.

And then a wonderful thing happened. The moment the ballerinas saw her, they began to smile. As their smiles grew, so did they, until they were as tall as real girls.

"Dear Bibi!" they exclaimed, racing to meet her.

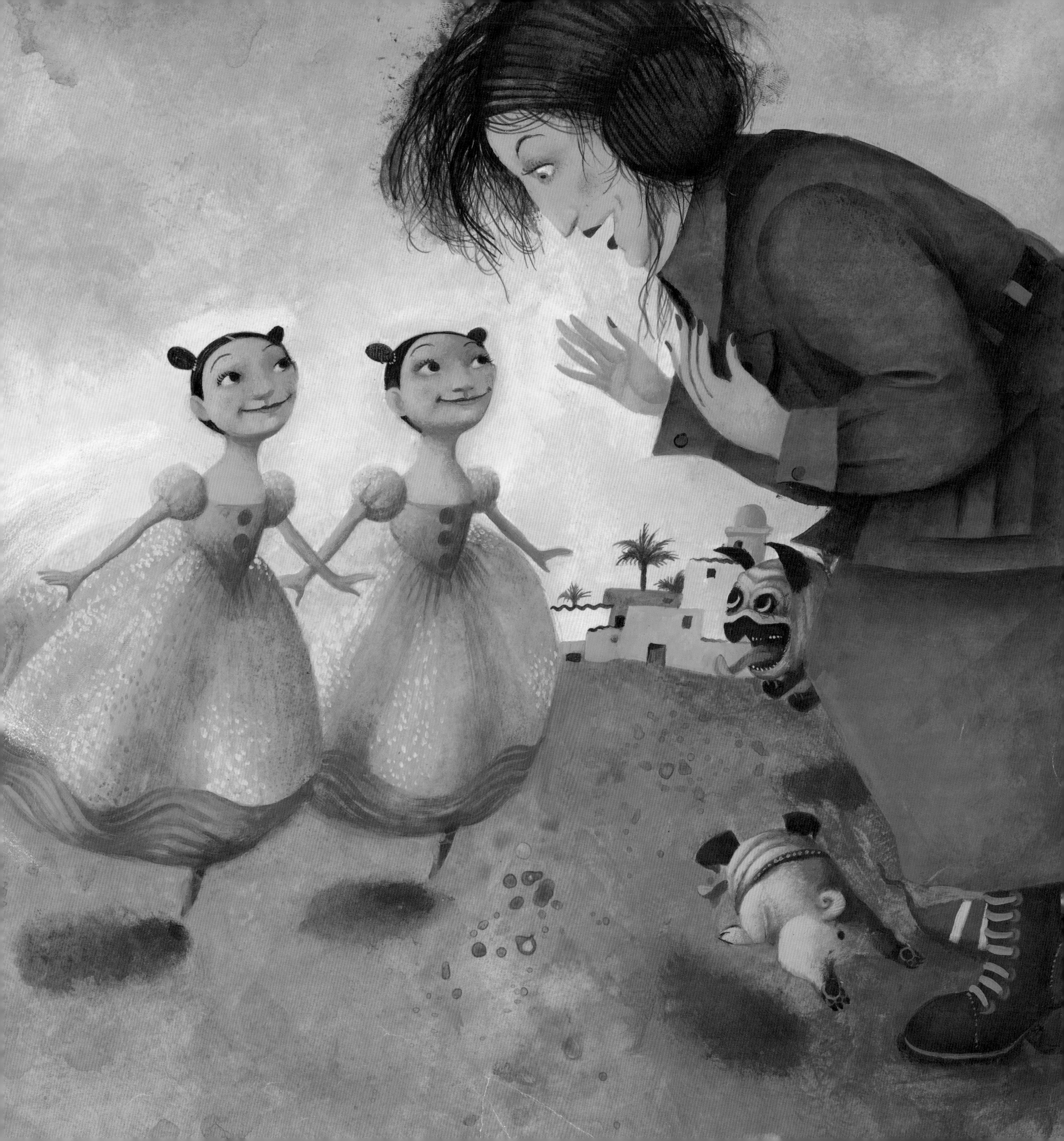

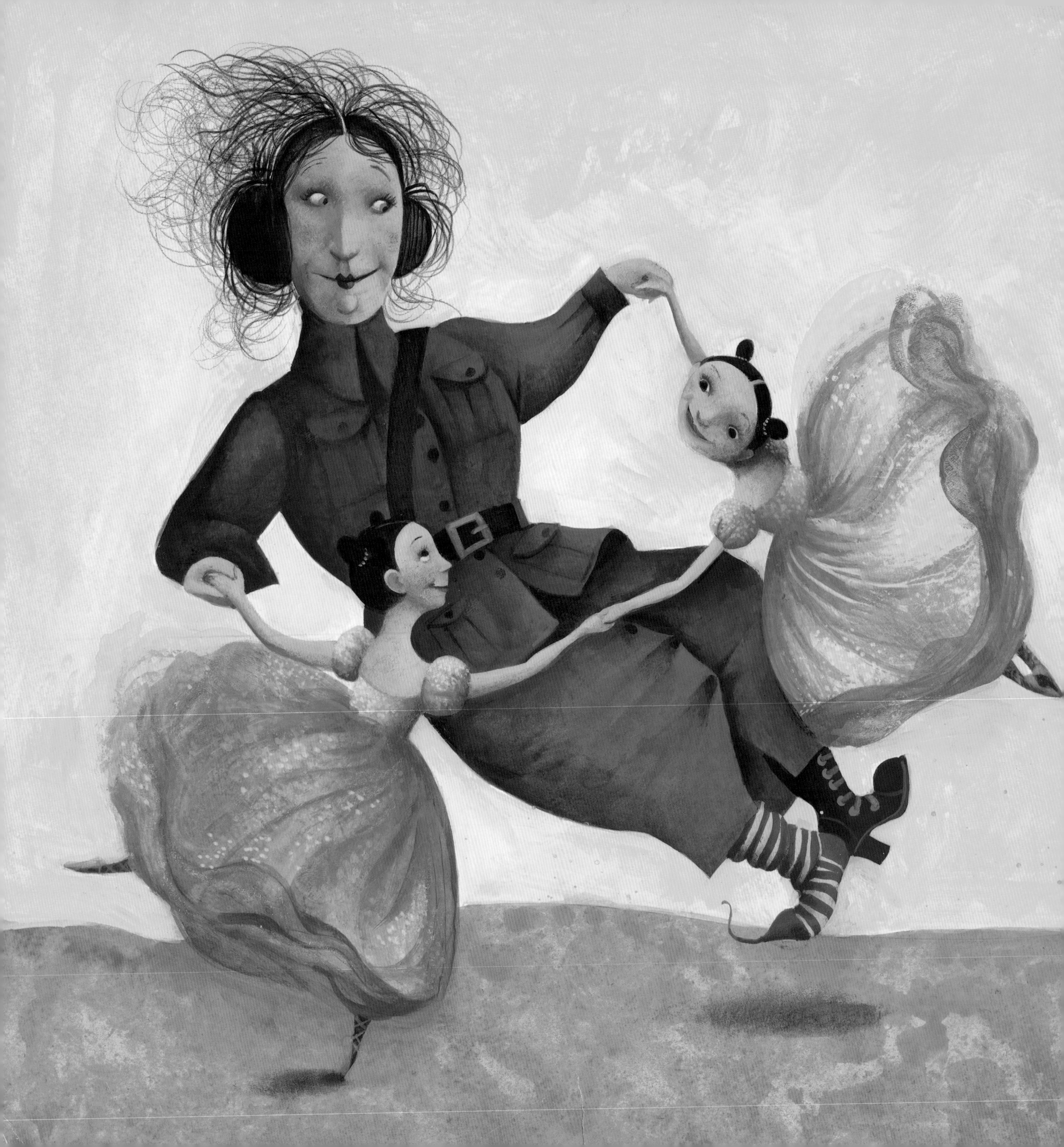

Miranda and Matilda caught Bibi's hands in theirs, and together, they leaped and whirled with joy.

"Now I have two friends—two wonderful friends!" cried Bibi as she clicked her heels in the air. "And I am happy, for that's all I need in the world."

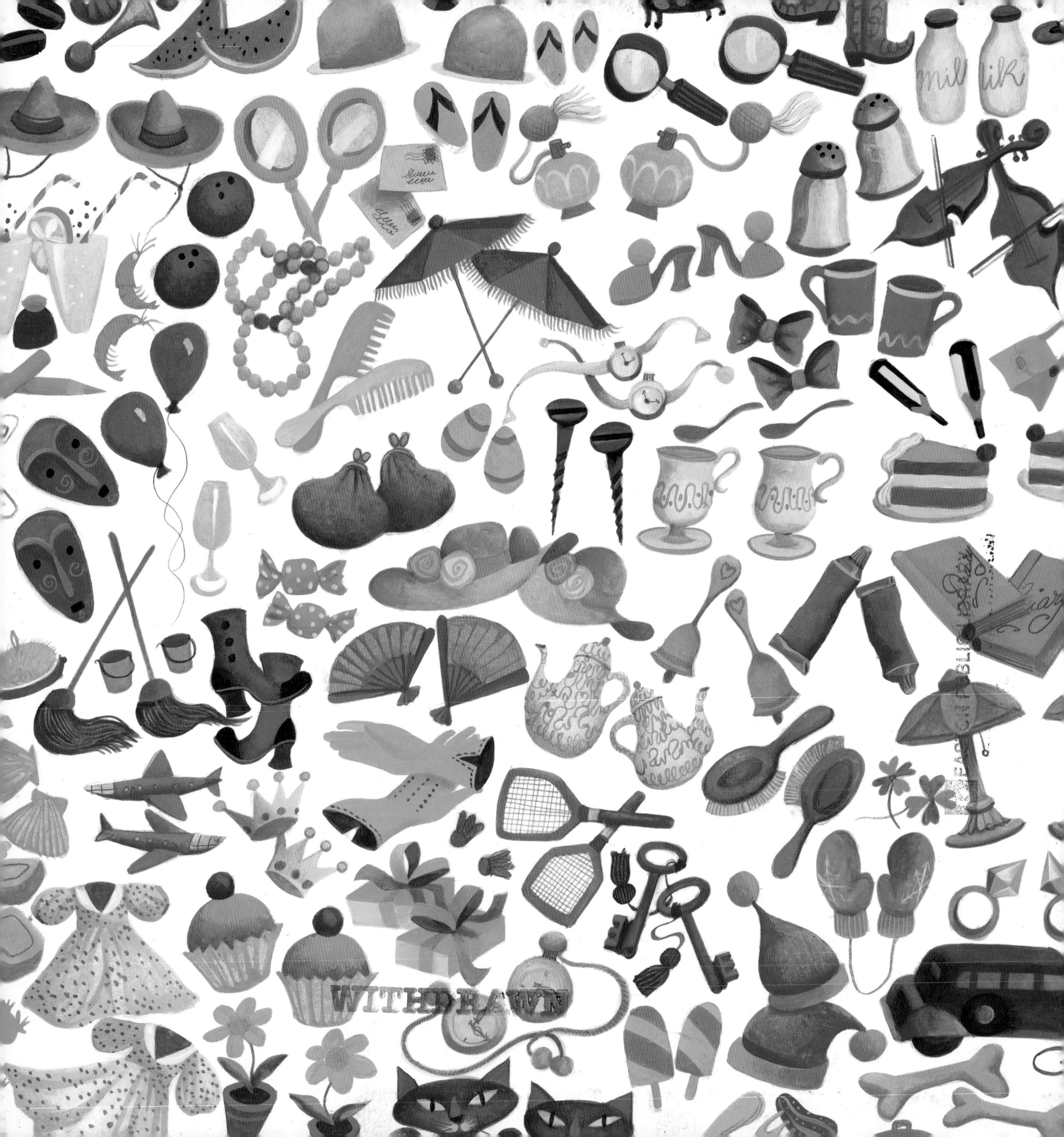